ISBN 1 85854 573 0
Published by Brimax Books Ltd, Newmarket,
England, CB8 7AU, 1997.
Printed in Spain.

Aesop's Fables

Adapted by Lucy Kincaid

Illustrated by Gill Guile

Brimax · Newmarket · England

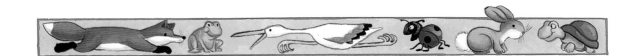

Aesop's Fables

Aesop was a Greek slave who lived thousands
of years ago. He was a very clever storyteller.
His stories are called fables. Each story has
a moral intended to teach us useful lessons.
We usually discover the moral after we have
read the story and think about it. The fables
of Aesop teach us as much today as they
taught the Ancient Greeks.

Contents

The Boy Who Cried Wolf

A shepherd boy looked after the sheep in the meadow. It was a lonely job, with no one to talk to. One day, the shepherd boy said, "What can I do to make things more interesting?" Suddenly he had an idea.

"WOLF!" he shouted. "There is a wolf among the sheep!"

The villagers heard the shouting and ran to the meadow to chase the wolf away. They ran around looking for the wolf. The shepherd boy laughed. There wasn't really a wolf - he had only pretended.

A few days later, the shepherd boy was bored again.

"WOLF!" he shouted, and once more, the villagers came running. When they couldn't find a wolf, they were angry.

"That boy is wasting our time by playing jokes," they said.

The next day, the villagers heard the shepherd boy for a third time. "WOLF!" he cried. But they ignored him.

This time there really was a wolf. It ran among all the sheep and killed them.

"Why didn't you help me chase the wolf away?" cried the shepherd boy to the villagers. "Now all the sheep are dead."

"You only have yourself to blame," said the villagers. "You should never have cried 'wolf' when there wasn't one. How were we to know there was really a wolf in the meadow?"

MORAL   *You should mean what you say.*

The Town Mouse and the Country Mouse

The Country Mouse invited the Town Mouse to visit him. He lived in a straw nest in a hedge and ate only corn. He put a clean tablecloth on the table and made his house tidy and snug. When the Town Mouse arrived, he nibbled at the corn on the table, but he didn't like it.

"You poor thing," said the Town Mouse to the Country Mouse. "You live in a tiny nest and eat only corn. Come to my house and have some proper food."

So the Country Mouse followed the Town Mouse into town.

The Town Mouse lived in a cupboard in a big house. The Country Mouse had never seen so much food before! There were raisins, cheese, chocolate and bread.

"Help yourself," said the Town Mouse.

The Country Mouse had just started to nibble on some cheese, when the cupboard door opened. A huge hand reached in and lifted out the cheese.

"Quick! Hide!" whispered the Town Mouse, pulling the Country Mouse into a hole at the back of the cupboard. The two mice shook with fear. When the door closed again the Town Mouse said, "It's safe to come out now."

So the mice crept out of the hole and began to eat some bread. Suddenly the cupboard opened again, and the Town Mouse pulled the Country Mouse back into the hole.

As soon as it was safe, the Country Mouse said, "I'm going home. I may only have corn to eat, but at least I can eat it without being frightened."

MORAL *Our own home always seems best to us.*

The Hare and the Tortoise

One day, Hare and Tortoise were arguing.

"I could beat you in a race, any day," Hare said to Tortoise.

"Hmm," said Tortoise. "Maybe you could."

"I could!" said Hare. "My legs can run much faster than yours."

"That doesn't mean you would win a race," said Tortoise.

"Then we should have a race," said Hare.

So the race was arranged. "I'll wait for you at the finishing post," shouted Hare to Tortoise, and he sped off.

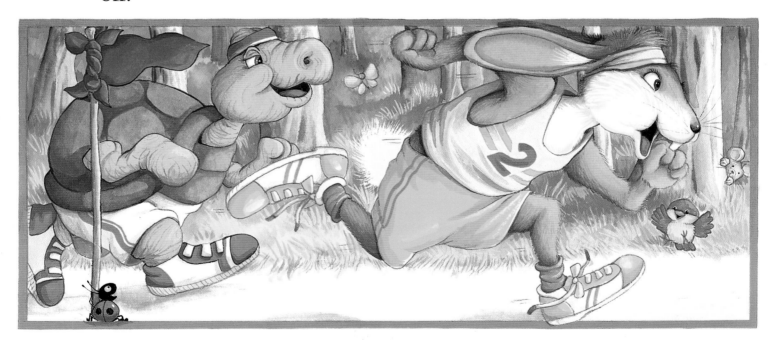

"Maybe," said Tortoise, and he plodded slowly after Hare.

"This is easy," said Hare to himself as he raced along.

After a while, Hare stopped and looked behind him. There was no sign of Tortoise. As it was very hot, Hare sat under a tree, in the shade. There was plenty of time, and Tortoise would never catch up with him. Hare closed his eyes.

After a while Tortoise reached the tree. He saw Hare sleeping under it. Hare didn't see Tortoise plodding by.

Later, Hare woke up and raced off to the finishing post. He couldn't believe it when he saw Tortoise waiting for him.

"You must have cheated!" said Hare to Tortoise.

"Certainly not!" said Tortoise. "While you were sleeping, I carried on with the race!"

MORAL *Keep your mind on a job until it is finished.*

The Fox and the Stork

One day, Fox went to visit Stork to invite her to dinner.

The next night, Stork arrived at Fox's house. "Something smells good," she said as she watched Fox making dinner.

"Come and eat then," said Fox. He looked at Stork's long, thin beak and smiled to himself.

Fox had made soup. He poured it into big, flat dishes. Fox began to lap from his dish. But Stork couldn't eat her soup. Her beak was too long and thin, and the dish was too flat. She was too polite to complain, and went home still hungry. Fox thought this was very funny.

Stork decided that Fox should be taught a lesson. She invited Fox to her house for dinner. Stork made soup, just as Fox had done. But this time the soup was served in tall, thin jugs, just the right size and shape for Stork to put her beak into.

Fox couldn't eat any of the soup. The jugs were too tall and thin. He went home in a bad mood because Stork had played the same joke on him.

MORAL *Something which is funny when it happens to someone else, may not be so funny if it happens to us.*

The Lion and the Mouse

One day, Mouse scampered over Lion's tail. Lion roared and put his huge paw over Mouse's tail.

"Please let me go!" squeaked Mouse.

"I'm going to eat you," roared Lion.

"If you let me go, I will find a way to help you one day."

Lion thought this was funny. How could a tiny mouse help him? He laughed at the mouse, and let him go.

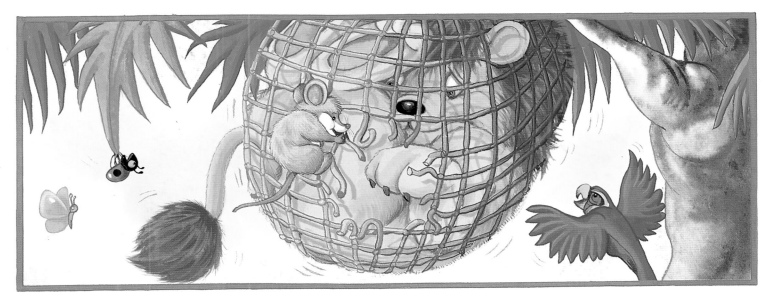

A few days later, some hunters captured Lion in a net. They tied the net to a tree so that Lion couldn't get away.

The ropes were very tight, and although he tried, Lion couldn't get free. Then he heard a tiny voice in his ear. It was Mouse.

"I will help you," squeaked Mouse.

"How can you help me?" asked Lion. "You are too small."

But Mouse began to chew at the ropes and net with his sharp teeth. Soon he had chewed right through them, and Lion was able to free himself. He thanked Mouse for his help.

"Now you can see how someone as small as me can help someone as big as you," said Mouse.

MORAL *Sometimes we can help, even if we are very small.*

A Wolf in Sheep's Clothing

Wolf was always hungry. There was nothing he liked to eat better than a fat sheep. He knew where there was a flock of sheep, and he had thought of a way to trick the shepherd. Then Wolf could have sheep for his dinner every night.

Wolf killed one sheep, and he pulled the sheepskin over his back like a coat. Then he crept into the middle of the flock when the shepherd wasn't looking.

"Baa, baa!" said Wolf. Even the sheep thought he was another sheep!

"I will wait until the shepherd goes for his dinner," said Wolf to himself. "Then I will have mine!"

The shepherd began to round up the sheep and put them into a pen. He didn't know there was a wolf in the pen, too.

But Wolf wasn't quite as clever as he thought he was. How was he to know that the shepherd was going to have sheep for his dinner, too? The shepherd picked out which sheep he was going to kill. It turned out to be the wolf in sheep's clothing. And that was the end of him!

MORAL *Clever tricks do not always work.*

The Greedy Fox

One day, a fox was looking for something to eat. He saw a shepherd putting something into a hole in a tree. Fox wondered what it might be. He waited until the shepherd went, then went to look in the tree.

Fox poked his nose into the hole and found the shepherd's dinner. Fox was so hungry, he squeezed into the hole and ate all of the food. It had been a long time since he had eaten such a big meal.

Fox thought he had been very clever. But then he tried to get out of the hole. He had eaten so much food, and his tummy had grown so fat, he was well and truly stuck!

"Help! Help!" cried Fox.

Another fox passing by heard the cries for help.

"What is wrong?" he asked.

When the passing fox was told he said, "There is only one thing you can do. You must wait until you are hungry and thin again, and then you will be able to get out."

MORAL *We should think about what might happen before we do something.*

The Birds, the Beasts and the Bat

Long ago, the birds and the beasts had a war. No one was sure how it started. The birds would fly at the beasts and pull out their fur, and the beasts would try to pull out the birds' feathers. Sometimes the birds would win the battles, and sometimes the beasts would win. But the bat was always on the winning side.

If it looked as if the birds were winning, the bat thought he was a bird too, and would join them. If the beasts were winning, the bat thought of himself as one of them. He changed sides many times.

Then one day, the war ended. The birds and beasts became friends. They decided to choose a king.

"I was always on the winning side," said the bat. "That proves how clever I am. I should be king."

"You! King!" said the birds and beasts together. "You were only willing to be on the winning side. When it seemed as if you would lose, you swapped sides."

Instead of making the bat king, the birds and beasts chased him from their kingdom.

MORAL *Real friends do not desert us when we are in trouble.*

The Bee-keeper and the Bees

The bee-keeper looked after the bees in his garden. They had a hive to live in and were safe from harm. The bees spent their days flying in and out of the hive, and making honey.

The bee-keeper loved honey. Whenever the bees made enough, he took some for himself. He never took too much, and the bees were happy because they were looked after.

One day, when all the bees were out of the hive and the bee-keeper wasn't at home, thieves broke into the hive. They stole all the honey. When the bee-keeper came home and saw the broken hive, he was very sad.

"The bees will be angry to see this," said the bee-keeper, and he began to mend the broken hive.

But the bees returned before the hive was mended. When they saw it, they thought the bee-keeper had ruined their home and taken all their honey. They began to sting the bee-keeper. They didn't ask how their home came to be broken.

"Stop! Stop!" cried the bee-keeper. "It wasn't me who did this!" But the bees didn't believe him.

The bee-keeper never kept bees again, and the bees lost a good friend.

MORAL *Ask questions before you act, or you may do something silly.*

The Boy and the Hazelnuts

One day, a boy saw his mother fill a jar with hazelnuts.

"May I have some nuts please?" the boy asked.

"Of course," said the boy's mother. "Help yourself."

The boy put his hand inside the jar and grabbed as many nuts as he could hold. But then, to his mother's surprise, the boy began to cry.

"What is wrong?" asked the boy's mother.

"My hand is stuck! I can't get it out," said the boy.

"Let me have a look," said his mother. Then she saw all the nuts he was holding.

"What shall I do?" sobbed the boy.

"Let go of half the nuts you are holding," said his mother.

When the boy did this, his hand came out of the jar easily.

"You were being greedy," said the boy's mother. Then she put the lid back on the jar, and put the jar on a high shelf.

MORAL *Do not try to take too much at one time.*

Jupiter and the Tortoise

The tortoise hasn't always carried his shell on his back. This is how it came about.

Jupiter was a powerful god. He invited all the animals to his wedding. The lion was there. The elephant was there. So were the rabbit and the mouse. Big or small, all the animals in the land were there... except for the tortoise.

"Where is Tortoise?" asked Jupiter, as he walked among the animals bowing before him. Nobody knew.

"Perhaps he is ill," said Elephant.

The next day, Jupiter went to look for Tortoise. He found him sitting outside his house, enjoying the sun.

"Were you ill yesterday?" Jupiter asked Tortoise.

"No," said Tortoise.

"Then why didn't you come to my wedding?" said Jupiter.

"I would rather be at home," said Tortoise thoughtlessly.

This made Jupiter very angry.

"If being at home means more to you than coming to my wedding, from now on you can carry your home with you wherever you go," said Jupiter.

And that is why the tortoise carries his home on his back.

MORAL *Think before you speak.*

The Grasshopper and the Ants

All through the summer the ants were busy looking for food to store in their pantry. The grasshopper watched them as he lay in the grass.

"Why are you working so hard?" he asked them. "You are not even eating the food you are finding. You should be like me and enjoy the sunshine. Leave all the work until winter."

The ants didn't listen to the grasshopper. And the grasshopper didn't listen to the ants when they said he should look for food to store in his pantry.

All summer, the grasshopper was very lazy, and he laughed at the ants who were working so hard.

Then winter arrived. The ants were snug inside their home. They didn't have to go outside into the cold and snow to look for food. They had all the food they needed in their pantry.

But the grasshopper didn't have any food. He tried to look for things to eat, but it was so cold and icy, there was little to be found. He wished that he had listened to the ants and had stored his food during the summer as they had done.

MORAL *We should always make plans for the future.*

The Eagle and the Beetle

An eagle flew over a hare, trying to catch him for dinner.

"Help!" cried the hare as he ran through the grass. But no one helped him.

"Stop that! Stop that at once!" shouted a tiny beetle at the eagle. "Leave that hare alone!"

But the eagle swooped down on the hare and ate it.

The beetle was very angry. She thought that the eagle should be punished. So the beetle kept watch on the eagle, and found out where she kept her nest. Every time the eagle laid an egg, the beetle rolled the egg over the edge of the nest so that it fell to the ground and broke.

The beetle broke so many of the eagle's eggs that the eagle went to see the god Jupiter. She asked if she could lay her eggs in his lap to keep them safe.

"You may," said Jupiter.

"My eggs will be safe from that beetle," said the eagle.

But the beetle went to see Jupiter. When he wasn't looking, the beetle placed some mud on Jupiter's lap. Without thinking, Jupiter stood up to brush away the mud. The eagle's eggs fell to the ground and smashed.

Ever since then, eagles have laid their eggs in high nests where they can't be found. This is why we hardly see them.

MORAL *Never stop trying.*

Jupiter and the Monkey

Jupiter called all the animals together. He said he would give a prize to the most beautiful baby animal in the land. All the baby animals were washed and brushed.

"Keep yourselves clean," said all the mother animals. "No playing in the mud until Jupiter has seen you."

Then all the animals stood in a line with their babies. Jupiter walked up and down, trying to decide who should have the prize. He patted the lion cub's head and stroked the tiger cub's nose. He smoothed the baby squirrel's tail.

"It is very difficult to choose," said Jupiter.

Then Jupiter stood in front of the monkey. Her baby had a tiny face with a flat nose, and no hair.

"What a funny baby," said Jupiter to the mother monkey. "Surely you did not think he would win the prize?"

"Of course I did," said the mother monkey. "He may look funny to you, but to me he is the most beautiful baby in the world."

Then Jupiter realized he couldn't give a prize to any of the baby animals.

"There will be no prize," he said. "Every baby is beautiful to its mother, and that is what is important."

MORAL *What seems beautiful to you may not seem beautiful to someone else.*

The Quack Frog

Frog was bored. He was tired of sitting beside the pond. He wanted to do something different.

"I know, I'll pretend I'm a doctor," said Frog. He filled some bottles with water and set up a stall in the market place. Although Frog wasn't really a doctor, he thought he could trick anyone into believing that he was.

"Come and see!" called Frog. "I have a potion for everything. Toothache, tummyache, headache, backache, spots! Whatever is wrong with you, I can make you better!"

Soon a crowd of animals gathered around Frog's stall.

"I'll have a bottle for my sore leg," said a cat.

"And I'll have one for my bad back," said a horse.

A fox watched this going on. He wasn't fooled by the frog.

"Can you make anything better?" asked the fox.

"Of course," said Frog.

"Then why is your own skin so blotchy and wrinkled and why do you hop instead of walk? Why haven't you made yourself better?" asked the fox.

The crowd grew silent. The cat tasted her potion.

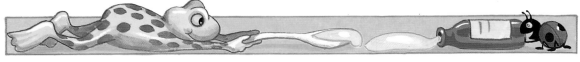

"It's water!" she cried. "I want my money back!"

"We all want our money back!" shouted the crowd.

As soon as the money was returned, Frog was chased out of town.

The Mice and the Weasels

The mice and the weasels were always fighting. The weasels were much bigger than the mice, and they beat them every time. The mice were tired of this. They called a meeting.

"Why are we always beaten?" they asked each other.

"Because we have no leaders," said one mouse.

So five mice were chosen to be generals.

"We must have helmets so that everyone knows who we are," they said.

So the generals wore heavy helmets with feathers in, and big badges around their necks. They felt important. Then the generals led the mice into another battle with the weasels.

"We'll show you how to frighten the weasels," they said.

But the weasels didn't run. They laughed instead.

"After them!" shouted the biggest weasel.

"Run for your lives!" shouted the mice, forgetting their generals. They dived into their holes where they were safe.

"Where are our generals?" said the mice, suddenly remembering.

The generals were dead. The heavy helmets had blocked the way into their holes, and the weasels had caught them.

"We're better off without generals if that is what happens to them," said the rest of the mice.

MORAL *What we do is more important than how we look.*

The Swan and the Crow

The crow spent a lot of time watching the swans swimming on the lake. He thought their white feathers and long necks were very beautiful.

The crow had shiny, black feathers and a strong beak. His wings could carry him into the sky. But he wasn't pleased with these things. He wanted to be like the swans. He wanted to swim on the lake and have white feathers and a long neck.

"If I try hard enough I can be a swan," said the crow.

He watched the swans and copied all they did. He left his home in the trees and lived by the lake. He learned how to swim, even though he didn't like the cold water.

He thought that if he scrubbed his feathers they would become white. Soon his feathers were torn. They weren't shiny any more, and they stayed as black as they had always been.

"It must be the food I am eating," said the crow.

He stopped eating his usual food, and ate the same food as the swans. But this made him ill. The crow grew very thin.

No matter what the crow did, he couldn't become a swan. At last he realized that nothing would change him. Instead of being happy with what he was, he had tried to change himself into something that he wasn't.

MORAL *Some things cannot be changed.*

The Ox and the Frogs

A family of frogs lived happily by a pond. The two youngest frogs spent hours playing with the other animals who lived there, and with the animals who came to drink the water.

One day a dreadful accident happened. A big ox came down to the pond for a drink. He was so big, he didn't see the two little frogs. As he made his way to the edge of the pond, he stepped on one of them and squashed him flat. The other frog went home to tell his mother what had happened.

"A great big animal stepped on my brother and killed him," said the little frog sadly.

"How big was this animal?" asked the frog's mother. "Was he as big as this?" And she puffed out her cheeks and sides.

"Oh, much, much bigger than that," said the little frog.

The frog's mother puffed and puffed and puffed. She made herself as big and round as a pumpkin.

"Was he as big as ..." she began - but then she burst.

MORAL *Sometimes it is better not to know something.*

The Dog and his Reflection

One day, a dog found a piece of meat. He picked it up in his mouth and set off for home. He held his head up high so that the meat didn't get dirty.

'Wait till my friends see this,' thought the dog to himself. 'What a big supper I will have tonight.'

On the way home, the dog had to cross a river. Usually he just splashed through the water, but today he used the bridge. The dog was half way across when he looked down into the water. He stopped. There was another dog looking up at him! And it was carrying an even bigger piece of meat!

'I want that piece of meat,' thought the dog to himself, and he dropped the one he was carrying, and jumped into the water to try to snatch the meat from the other dog.

"Where has it gone?" howled the dog.

The meat and the other dog had disappeared. All he could see were ripples and splashes, and his own piece of meat floating down the river.

The silly dog had been looking at his own reflection. He thought it was another dog with a bigger piece of meat. Because he had been so greedy, he had no supper at all.

MORAL *We should be happy with what we have.*